Weekly Reader Children's Book Club presents

The Happy Dromedary

Printed in the United States of America/Library of Congress Catalog Card Number 76-1323/ISBN 0-684-14853-6

3 5 7 9 11 13 15 17 19 RD/C 20 18 16 14 12 10 8 6 4 2

Weekly Reader Children's Book Club Edition

The Happy Dromedary

by Berniece Freschet   illustrated by Glen Rounds

Charles Scribner's Sons / New York

Millions and millions of years ago, when the birds and beasts first came upon the earth, the King of the Animals said:

4

"Go and look throughout the land and find a place to
live—for you may make your home wherever you choose."

5

The leopard and the tiger chose to live in the leafy jungle.

The bear and the wolf chose the cool, shady forest.

The rabbit and the mouse chose the grassy meadow.

And the birds chose the trees and the air above the earth
in which to make their home.

Not many creatures wanted to live in the hot, sandy desert.

But when the dromedary went out into the world to find her place and came to the desert, she said,

"This is where I want to live. Here in the beautiful desert—where the eye can see from horizon to horizon—where there is no sound but silence...

...and where no snow falls to chill my body, and no cold winds blow to weaken my bones."

But in the beginning the dromedary, also called camel, did not look the same as she does today, and when she tried to walk upon the desert, her feet sank into the sand.

So the dromedary went to the King of the Animals and she said, "Oh, great King. I want to live in the beautiful desert where the sky is as blue as the blue, blue sea, and where the morning sun turns the hills of sand from pink to gold.

"But my feet are so small that when I try to walk upon the desert they sink into the sand and I cannot go far. Please— would you make my feet bigger?"

"As you wish," said the busy Animal King, and the great King changed the dromedary's feet—making them large, and flat, and floppy.

And the dromedary was very happy.

She went back to the desert. Now she could walk upon the sand. PLOP—PLOP—PLOP! went her large, flat feet.

16

But the way was far between the water holes. And soon the dromedary became hungry and thirsty.

So she went to the Animal King and she said,
    "Oh, great King. Now I can walk upon the sand, but the way is far between the water holes, and I soon get hungry and thirsty. Please, would you give me a large hump on my back to store food and water?"

18

And the tired King said, "As you wish." He gave the dromedary a large hump on her back to store food and water.

And the dromedary was very happy. Now she could walk upon the sand with her large, flat feet—and she could go long distances without food or water.

But the other animals laughed at her.

"Look at those funny, floppy feet," said the goat.

"Look at that lumpy hump on her back," said the horse.

"Look how UGLY she is!" cried the tortoise.

The dromedary was very sad.

She went to the King of the Animals again. "Oh, great
King," she said. "Now the others call me ugly, and they laugh
at the way I look. Please change me back to the way I was
before."

And the Animal King said, "You came to me and asked for large, flat feet to walk upon the desert sand, and I gave them to you. Then you asked for a large hump on your back to store food and water, and I gave you that. Now you come and ask me to undo all that I have done—that even I cannot do."

The Animal King turned away.

"Go," he said. "I have much work to finish. Do not bother me again."

The unhappy dromedary hung her head. She went away
and hid from the other animals. She wouldn't eat—she wouldn't
drink.

She just sat and thought.

More than anything else, the dromedary wanted to live in the golden desert, but it made her sad when the others laughed at the way she looked. After much thought, she finally decided that she must go away and find a new place to live.

Her head bent low, she plodded slowly back to the Animal King.

"I'm sorry to trouble you again, great King, but I must leave the beautiful desert. I cannot be happy there where everyone laughs at me."

The Animal King looked up with weary eyes.

"Dromedary," he said, "no other animal was clever enough to think of the special gifts that you thought of for living in the desert. You must not leave, for you will be a most valuable friend to the people who one day will come to live there."

Then the tired King closed his eyes and for a long while was silent. Just as the dromedary had decided that he must have fallen asleep, the Animal King opened his eyes.

"Hummmmm—I have an idea. I'll just make your neck longer and push back your nose a bit—that should do it."

And when he was done he told the dromedary,

"Now go and live in your beautiful desert—and be happy."

When next the dromedary met the other animals, she lifted her long neck high. Her chin went up, and she sniffed. She pretended that she didn't see the others.

At first the animals laughed—but then a strange thing happened. As they stood looking up at the tall dromedary, one by one, they stopped laughing.

"How very proud she looks," said the goat.
"And so important," said the horse.

"She *is* important," said the tortoise. "No other animal can walk as far across the hot desert without tiring as she, or travel as many days without food or water."
"My," sighed the animals, "how great and beautiful she is."

And so it is, with her long neck stretched high, and her chin tilted up toward the sky, the happy dromedary walks across her golden desert—

PLOP—PLOP—PLOP!